SPACE
SCOOTER

BRENT FILSON

Illustrated by Mark Kaplan

Copyright © 1989, 1980 by Brent Filson.
All rights reserved. Published by Scholastic Inc.
SPRINT and SPRINT BOOKS are trademarks of Scholastic Inc.
Printed in the U.S.A.
ISBN 0-590-35165-6

2 3 4 5 6 7 8 9 10   31   03 02 01 00 99 98 97 96

CHAPTER 1

Dust flew up as Sam's scooter landed. Sam's scooter was new. Mine was old. Sam took off his bubble. He waved to the people. Then he looked at my scooter and laughed.

"Give up, Billy," he said. "You don't have a chance against me. Your scooter is no good."

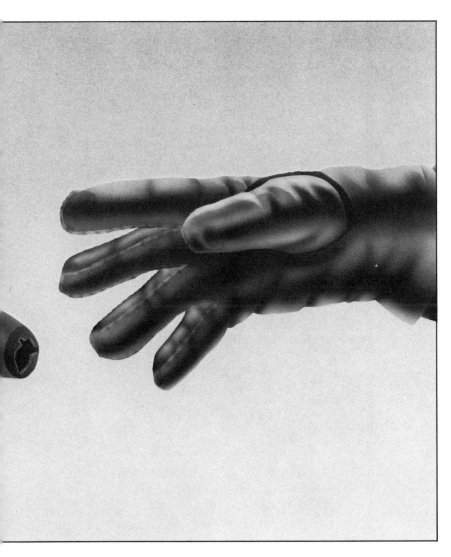

He reached over to touch my scooter with his new glove. Everything Sam owned was new. Sam, like all the other people on Venus, was rich. I pushed his hand away.

"I was only trying to be friendly," he laughed.

"My scooter will do the job," I said. "I made it from old parts. That's the way we people on Earth do things."

Sam laughed again. "You Earth people never do things right."

Just then a voice called out, "THIS RACE

WILL BE ONCE AROUND VENUS. THICK CLOUDS COVER THE DESERT. READY. SET. GO!"

I pushed my power stick. My scooter took off. The people below suddenly got smaller and smaller. We were off to a fast start!

CHAPTER 2

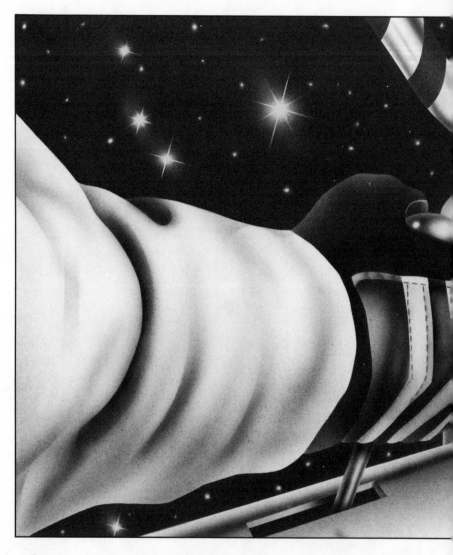

I saw new cities below me. The cities were covered with large bubbles. The bubbles kept dangerous clouds out.

One hundred years ago, in the year 2030, people left Earth. They came to Venus. They left old cities to live in new cities. People who

could not pay for the ride stayed on Earth. I was visiting Venus for the summer. I had won the trip in a contest.

I pushed my stick to Power Five. That was my scooter's fastest speed. I wanted to show these people what an Earth scooter could do.

BANG! My scooter shook. Smoke shot out of my engine. I was losing speed. I saw Sam suddenly fly by me. He was laughing at me. I had made a big mistake. I had gone into Power Five too soon. My engine was not warmed up.

I had to fix that engine if I wanted to win. I knew I had to work fast. My engine door was on the side of my scooter. But as I opened the door, there was another bang. Smoke poured into my face. My scooter was going down!

CHAPTER 3

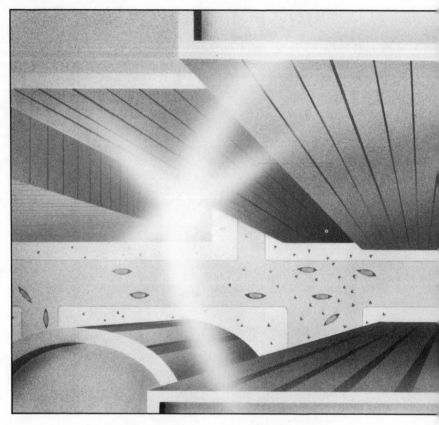

My engine was dead. I had to work fast. The ground was getting close. I pulled a bad part out of the engine. I put a good part in its place. I closed the door and turned on the engine.

The engine came on. The scooter stopped spinning. But it was still headed straight for the ground. Right under me was a city!

I pulled hard on the stick. The nose of the scooter went up a little. But the city was getting very close. I could see people on the streets. They were running for cover. They

thought I was going to crash.

I pulled as hard as I could on the stick. I held my breath and pushed the engine to Power Five. The nose came up a little more. I felt my scooter jump. I was going up! I had just missed the bubble cover of the city. A few more inches and I would have hit it. But my scooter was going up, fast. I let out my breath. I wiped my face. It was a close call. But I did not have any time to be scared. I had to get back into the race!

19

CHAPTER 4

My fuel needle was dropping to empty. But I kept it at Power Five. I was going to catch Sam — or blow my scooter to pieces!

I spotted Sam up ahead. I pulled beside him. He looked angry. I saw him push his stick hard. But he gave it too much power too fast.

His scooter started shaking. I saw a flash.
Smoke came out of the back. Then it started
dropping out of sight. It was smoking badly.

I turned my scooter around and followed
Sam's smoke trail. The smoke went down
through clouds. Then I saw the scooter. It had

landed on the desert floor. It was still in one piece. I landed right next to it.

Sam was standing by his scooter. He was not laughing now. He was shaking all over. He was scared. "Boy, am I glad to see you," he said. "I thought it was all over for me."

I looked at his scooter. "Here is your problem," I said. "A broken engine part. I had the same problem." I put his engine back together.

"Let's go!" Sam yelled. He ran for his scooter. "We have to get back in the race!"

CHAPTER 5

We ran toward our scooters. But suddenly I could not see. A thick cloud had blown down on us. Sam and I bumped against each other. I fell down. I crawled through the blowing sand. I saw a black shape. It was a scooter. I got on it and took off.

When we got out of the cloud, I saw what

had happened. Up ahead was MY scooter. Sam
was on it. And I was on HIS scooter. We had
gotten mixed up in the storm cloud. We were on
the wrong scooters!

Sam raced toward the finish line. I put his
scooter on full power. But I could not catch my
scooter. He sailed across the finish line, first.

Dust flew up as he landed. He jumped off the scooter and threw up his hands. "I win!" he yelled.

I went over the finish line. The scooter was smoking. I jumped off. "MY scooter won!"

A voice called out, "IT IS A TIE. YOU BOTH

WIN. EARTH WINS. VENUS WINS. GIVE THE WINNERS A BIG HAND."

As the people clapped, Sam and I looked at each other. We laughed. We shook hands. We were not angry now. How can you be angry when you are a space scooter winner?